Biographies

和平抗爭
Mahatma Gandhi and Cesar Chavez

Anne Schraff

Development: Kent Publishing Services, Inc.

Design and Production: Signature Design Group, Inc.

Photo Credits: pages 23, 56 Zarchive, Zkeystone;

page 96, Wayne State University Library;

page 107, Library of Congress; page 119, David Bacon;

page 127, courtesy of the United States Post Office

書　　名：和平抗爭 Mahatma Gandhi and Cesar Chavez

作　　者：Anne Schraff

責　　編：黃家麗　王朴真

封面設計：張　毅

出　　版：商務印書館 (香港) 有限公司

　　　　　香港筲箕灣耀興道 3 號東滙廣場 8 樓

　　　　　http://www.commercialpress.com.hk

發　　行：香港聯合書刊物流有限公司

　　　　　香港新界大埔汀麗路 36 號中華商務印刷大廈 3 字樓

印　　刷：中華商務彩色印刷有限公司

　　　　　香港新界大埔汀麗路 36 號中華商務印刷大廈 14 字樓

版　　次：2012 年 11 月第 1 版第 1 次印刷

　　　　　©2012 商務印書館 (香港) 有限公司

　　　　　ISBN 978 962 07 1971 4

　　　　　Printed in Hong Kong

CONTENTS 目錄

Part 2
Cesar Chavez 凱薩・查維斯

Exercises 練習

Publisher's Note
出版說明

　　繼出版以漫畫為主的 Graphic Biography 系列後，商務印書館推出 Biographies 系列。新系列從 *TIME* magazine 二十世紀最具影響力的名人中，精選了不同領域的十位名人，有科學家愛因斯坦、前美國總統羅斯福、民權領袖馬丁・路德・金，還有勇於突破局限的海倫・凱勒。

　　Biographies 系列經 Saddleback Educational Publishing 授權出版。本系列增加 Cultural Note（文化知識點），介紹相關社會背景；附帶練習題，可供讀者掌握生詞和英語語法點。

　　"淺顯易懂、啟發心智"是為特點。我們衷心希望，本系列能為初級英語程度的讀者提供閱讀和學習的樂趣。

商務印書館（香港）有限公司

編輯出版部

Usage Note
使用說明

Step 1

通讀傳記故事。遇到生詞可即時參考註釋。若不明白故事背景，可閱讀文化知識點。

Step 2

完成練習題。若未能回答練習題，或回答錯誤時，可再查閱傳記相關內容。通過練習熟悉生詞意義和用法，掌握語法知識。

Step 3

閱讀中英對照生詞表，檢查是否已掌握生詞。尚未掌握的生詞，可重新閱讀傳記相關部分。

Step 4

閱讀人物年表，重溫傳記故事。讀者可模仿年表，用簡單詞句概括重要事件，練習撮要技巧。

Step 5

延伸閱讀列出有參考價值的相關書籍，讀者可按興趣深入閱讀。

Part 1

Mahatma Gandhi

穆罕達默·甘地

Family and childhood 家庭與童年

Mahatma Gandhi led the struggle for Indian independence from the British Empire. The British ruled India for many years. Gandhi also gained civil rights for the Indian population that lived in South Africa.

Although Gandhi was a small, frail[1] man, he faced strong nations using only his weapons of nonviolent resistance[2]. Encouraging all people to be kind, honest, and peaceful, Gandhi refused to return injury with injury.

1　frail, *adj*: 體弱
2　nonviolent resistance: 非暴力抵抗

Gandhi had no wealth and no political position. He fought injustice with prayer, fasting[1], and peaceful protest.

When Gandhi died, a young African American college student far away in the American South read about Gandhi's methods of bringing peaceful change. His name was Martin Luther King Jr. When King led his own struggle for the equality of black America, he walked in Gandhi's footsteps[2].

Mohandas Karamchand Gandhi was born on October 2, 1869. He was born in the small town of Porbandar on the western coast of India. Mohandas was born in a large room in the family's three-storey[3] stone house. Mohandas and his family lived in the big house. Several uncles and their families lived there too. Mohandas and his family had just two rooms for themselves.

---

1   fasting, *n*: 絕食
2   walk in sb's footsteps: 步某人後塵
3   three-storey: 三層，[美] three-story

Mohandas' father, Karamchand Gandhi, was a government official in town. He had been married three times, and each of his wives died. When he was forty, he married a fourth wife. She was thirteen-year-old Putlibai, Mohandas' mother. It was very common for older Indian men to marry very young brides. When Mohandas was born, his mother was twenty-two and his father was fifty.

The Gandhi family was comfortable by Indian standards. The home had many books, mostly about religion. The Gandhi family was Hindu, as were most Indians. The Hindu religion* is very complicated. It embraces a belief[1] in many gods and strict moral values.

Mohandas was a strange looking little boy. He had a long, skinny neck, and ears that stuck out[2]. He had wild, thick black hair. His best features were a happy smile, and bright, twinkling

*Cultural Note

Hindu religion：印度教。信仰多神、崇尚苦修、種姓分立，強調因果輪迴。

1   embrace a belief: 信奉
2   stick out: 凸出

eyes. Mohandas liked to play with rubber balloons and spinning tops[1]. He was small for his age and easily scared. He was afraid of snakes, thieves, ghosts, and the dark. He disliked all sports.

At the time Mohandas was born, India was ruled by Great Britain. The culture was dominated by the caste system*. Everything that happened to a person in life depended on what caste they belonged to. Your caste decided what job you could get and who you could marry. There were four major castes. At the very bottom, there was a group of people called the "untouchables". They were given the dirtiest jobs. They could not walk on the public streets, or even touch other people.

The top caste was the Brahmans, who were scholars. Then, there were the warriors[2]. After that came the traders, and finally the peasants[3]. The Gandhi

*Cultural Note

caste system：種姓制度，是印度的社會體系，將人分五個階級，由上至下是婆羅門(學者)、煞帝利(武士)、吠舍(商人)、首陀羅(農民)與賤民。

---

1   spinning top: 陀螺，美 revolving top
2   warrior, *n*: 武士
3   peasant, *n*: 農民

family belonged to the trader class. The name Gandhi means "grocer[1]". These people could also work for the government, as Mohandas' father did.

When Mohandas was seven, his father was promoted to a job in Rajkot, 120 miles from Porbandar. Mohandas started primary school there. He had problems with arithmetic. Mohandas made no friends in school, preferring to play alone. When Mohandas went to high school, he disliked it even more than he had disliked primary school.

Mohandas' mother, Putlibai, was very religious. She never ate a meal without praying first. She went to the Hindu temple every day. Putlibai had a strong, quiet personality. Mohandas loved her dearly. She was loving and tender[2] toward her children. Like most Indian women, she wore heavy silver anklets

---

1   grocer, *n*: 商人
2   tender, *adj*: 溫柔

and gold bracelets. She also wore a nice nose ring for special occasions.

Mohandas' father was a serious, hard-working man. Mohandas feared making him angry. Although it is against Hindu custom to smoke cigarettes, Mohandas sneaked[1] some cigarettes one day. Then he stole money to get more cigarettes.

He felt so guilty about what he had done that he decided he should kill himself. He collected seeds from a datura plant[2] and ate them. Then he lay down to die. The seeds, however, only made him sleepy.

Sometimes Mohandas went with his mother to the Hindu temple. The inside of the temple was very dark. The paintings on the walls were dramatic[3] and frightening. But Mohandas loved his mother so much he would do anything she asked of him.

---

1   sneak, *v*: 偷取
2   datura plant: 曼陀羅屬植物
3   dramatic, *adj*: 誇張

Sympathizing with the untouchables
同情賤民階級

When Mohandas was thirteen, he began to ask questions about things that bothered him. He could not understand why the untouchables*[1] were treated so badly just because they were born in a lower social position.

At this time in India, there was no indoor plumbing. (This was the case in many places throughout the world.) People used chamber pots[2] in their rooms, and somebody had to empty them. This was a job only the

*Cultural Note

the untouchables: 賤民階級，印度種姓制度中最低階級，只能做非常卑賤的行業，不能與其他階級通婚。

1　the untouchables: 賤民階級
2　chamber pot: 夜壺

untouchables could do. Mohandas watched the untouchables doing this. He thought it was not fair. Why should these people have the worst jobs and the least pay? Mohandas believed that the untouchables were just as good as he was.

Child marriage* was customary[1] in India. So, when Mohandas turned thirteen, his father decided he should get married. Mohandas was still in high school. After his marriage, he would continue to live at home, but his wife would be with him.

Mohandas and other boys his age did not make friends with girls and choose someone they liked. The marriages were arranged by the parents. So Mohandas was told he would be marrying Kasturba Nakanji. She was the daughter of a Porbandar merchant. Like Mohandas, Kasturba was thirteen.

*Cultural Note

child marriage: 童婚，指兒童或成年男性與女童的婚禮，是印度傳統習俗之一。由於嚴重影響兒童接受教育的權利與人權，印度政府已頒佈法令規定女性合法結婚年齡為 18 歲，但在鄉村或偏遠地區仍可見童婚習俗。

---

1   customary, *adj*: 按慣例

Mohandas was excited about the wedding and the big feast that would follow. Mohandas was dressed up like a prince. He rode a beautiful horse to Kasturba's house to pick her up for the ceremony[1]. Then the two young people stood on a platform looking like pretty dolls. The Hindu priests prayed and sang hymns[2]. The couple exchanged sweet cakes. They were now man and wife. Mohandas took Kasturba home to his parents' house.

Kasturba was still a young girl. She wanted to go out to play with her friends, but Mohandas was very stern[3]. He told her she needed his permission to go out at all. He was still in school and lived with his parents. But Mohandas understood what it was to be a Hindu husband. He was the ruler of the household.

---

1   ceremony, *n*: 典禮
2   hymn, *n*: 聖歌
3   stern, *adj*: 嚴厲

Kasturba was tiny and delicate and very lovely. Mohandas was jealous of her. When she disobeyed him in even a small way, he grew very angry. Now that Mohandas was married, his grades slipped in high school. He was too busy watching over[1] his wife to study.

At age fifteen, Mohandas became friends with a Muslim* boy who was three years older than him. Sheikh Mehtab had all the qualities Mohandas admired. Mehtab was charming[2] and brave. He was a fine athlete. Mehtab enjoyed the fact that Mohandas looked up to him. He taught the younger boy his own ideas.

Hindus, including Mohandas and his family, were vegetarians[3]. They did not believe in eating meat. But Mehtab, a Muslim, believed that eating the flesh of animals made a person strong and healthy.

*Cultural Note

Muslim: 穆斯林，泛指伊斯蘭教信徒。伊斯蘭教是以古蘭經和聖訓為教導的一神論宗教，唯一的神是真主阿拉。目前為世界第二大宗教。

1　watch over: 監督
2　charming, *adj*: 有魅力
3　vegetarian, *n*: 素食者

Mehtab finally convinced[1] Mohandas to eat meat. They shared a meal of roasted goat. Mohandas felt very guilty about acting against his religion. He threw up[2] the meal right away.

That night Mohandas had a horrible nightmare. He dreamt a live goat was trapped inside his stomach, and it was crying. But, even after this bad experience, Mohandas continued to eat meat with Mehtab. Mohandas got used to it and stopped feeling guilty.

Karamchand Gandhi, Mohandas' father, became very ill when his son was sixteen. After school every day, Mohandas went to his father's bedside. But, Mohandas wanted to go to his wife instead. He felt the duty to be with his father, but his heart was with Kasturba. At the time, Kasturba was expecting the couple's first child.

1　convince, *v*: 説服
2　throw up: 嘔吐

One day, Mohandas found his father sleeping, and he hurried off to his wife for a short time. While Mohandas was gone, his father grew sicker and died. It was a terrible shock[1] for Mohandas. He was very sorrowful[2] that his father died without his son at his bedside. Mohandas was torn with guilt that he had failed his father. A few weeks later, Kasturba gave birth to their child, but it was very weak.

The baby lived only three days. Mohandas blamed[3] himself for the baby's death. He believed he was suffering this misfortune because he had abandoned[4] his father in his time of sickness.

---

1   shock, *n*: 震驚
2   sorrowful, *adj*: 悲傷
3   blame, *v*: 責備
4   abandon, *v*: 拋棄

Turning point 人生轉捩點

The death of Karamchand Gandhi was a major blow[1] to the family. It left them without financial support. The eldest son, Laxmidas, was twenty-two years old, and he had no job. Mohandas had two more years of high school to finish. The family had to struggle[2] to keep Mohandas in school. They had to rely on the help of uncles.

In January 1888 Mohandas was eighteen. He had finished high school

---

1　blow, *n*: 打擊
2　struggle, *v*: 奮鬥

and enrolled[1] in college. He failed college after five months. Kasturba gave birth to[2] their first healthy child, Harilal. Mohandas could not support his wife and son. He decided to find a profession that would bring in good money. He chose law.

Mohandas Gandhi was told that he could become a lawyer if he went to Great Britain and studied for three years. This was less time than it would have taken him to become a lawyer in India. But the cost of this education in Great Britain was thirteen thousand rupees. That was a huge amount for a boy from a poor family. There were no scholarships[3].

Putlibai, Gandhi's mother, did not want her son to go to Britain. She worried that he would make friends with the wrong people and lose his

---

1   enroll, *v*: 註冊

2   give birth to: 誕下

3   scholarship, *n*: 獎學金

morality[1]. She feared he would drink spirits[2] and eat meat. She was afraid that he would even forget about his wife and find other women.

Gandhi promised his mother that all the time he would be in Britain he would not eat meat, drink liquor, or look at other women. So Laxmidas sold all the family jewels to give his brother enough money to be educated in Britain.

There was still another problem with Gandhi going to Britain. According to his religion, he was forbidden to ride on an ocean liner. So, when he decided to go anyway, he was excommunicated[3] from the Hindu religion.

Gandhi's family was not even allowed to go down to the dock and say goodbye to him. If they did they would also be thrown out of the Hindu religion. So,

---

1 morality, *n*: 道德
2 spirits, *n*: 酒，[美] liquor
3 excommunicate, *v*: 逐出

all alone, Gandhi boarded the S. S. Clyde bound for London. He was eighteen years old. He had nothing but his ticket, a few pieces of clothing, and enough food for the three week long journey to Britain.

Gandhi in South Africa where he was an attorney.
甘地在南非當律師。

Study in London 留學倫敦

Gandhi arrived in London and stayed with another Indian student. He used the money he had to buy some clothing so he would look like the English students. He wanted to fit in[1] when he arrived at London University for his classes.

Gandhi remembered his promise to his mother that he would be a strict[2] vegetarian, so he lived on meals of bread and vegetables. He lived a very simple

---

1　fit in: 適應
2　strict, *adj*: 嚴格

life. Each night he added up[1] everything he had spent during the day on bus fare, food, postage, and other items.

He kept trying to cut corners[2] and save money because he had so little. He decided he was spending too much money on bus fares, so he moved closer to the university, and each day he walked eight to ten miles to and from classes.

Gandhi cooked his own breakfast of cocoa and oatmeal. His lunch consisted of[3] vegetables. For dinner he had cocoa and bread and sometimes boiled spinach. Gandhi was very lonely and homesick during his time in London. The only pleasure he had was occasionally[4] eating at a small vegetarian restaurant near where he studied.

In college, Gandhi studied French, Latin, and physics as well as common

---

1 add up: 合計
2 cut corners: 一切從簡
3 consist of: 組成
4 occasionally, *adv*: 偶然

and Roman law. He improved his English. He had no trouble passing all his courses. In his free time, he continued his study of religion.

Up until the time he was in London, Gandhi had never read the sacred scripture[1] of his own Hindu religion: the Bhagavad-Gita*. Now he read it. He learned that to be good, a man must be generous and overcome[2] pride, fear, and ambition. Gandhi read the Christian Bible too. He loved the New Testament, especially the life of Jesus. He paid close attention[3] to the Sermon on the Mount. He found its message of love and forgiveness very powerful.

In June 1891 Gandhi finished his final exam. The next day he left London. He did not want to spend a single day longer than necessary in London. He did not enjoy the two years and eight

---

1　scripture, *n*: 經文

2　overcome, *v*: 克服

3　pay close attention: 很留心

months he spent there. He had not made a single friend, and he was anxious[1] to see his family.

When Gandhi arrived in Bombay (a city now known as Mumbai), he was met by his brother, Laxmidas, with terrible news. Their mother had died some time earlier. The news had been kept from Gandhi. They were afraid that he would be so heart-broken he would quit school. Gandhi was deeply attached to his mother. Now, grieving for[2] his mother, Gandhi set out to find work in India.

---

1   anxious, *adj*: 渴望
2   grieve for: 為⋯悲傷

Working in South Africa
南非工作經驗

Gandhi discovered that India was full of lawyers and there was no need for him. He spent many desperate[1] days looking for work. While at home, he tried to teach his wife a skill she had never learned—how to read and write. But she resisted his efforts[2].

Laxmidas and the rest of the family were disappointed that Gandhi was not finding work. In October 1892 a second son, Manilal, was born to Gandhi and

---

1   desperate, *adj*: 絕望
2   resist sb's efforts: 抵抗某人的努力

his wife. Now Gandhi had a wife and two children to support. Gandhi did a few odd jobs working with other lawyers. He made some money. But he knew he could not go on like this without steady income.

Then he got an offer to go to South Africa to help a Muslim lawyer prepare a lawsuit[1]. Gandhi hated to leave his family again, but he had no choice. Leaving his wife and sons with Laxmidas, Gandhi set out for Durban, South Africa, in April 1893.

South Africa was a large country ruled by Great Britain. The largest population was black Africans, and they had almost no rights. The British were at the top of the social system. At the bottom were the Africans. In the middle but near the bottom were Asians, mostly Indians. They had come to South Africa to work as laborers.

---

1 lawsuit, *n*: 訴訟

The white people included the ruling British and the Afrikaners*, or Boers. The Boers were Dutch. Both the British and the Boers agreed on the idea that people of color were inferior[1].

Since Gandhi was very dark skinned, he soon ran into trouble in South Africa. Colored people were not allowed to ride with white people on the trains. They had to use a separate compartment. When Gandhi was told this, he refused to ride the train at all.

The Muslim lawyer with whom Gandhi worked was Dada Abdulla. One day, Gandhi went to court with him. The judge asked Gandhi to remove his black turban*[2]. Gandhi refused and said he was insulted[3]. He left the courtroom rather than remove his turban.

When Gandhi tried the train again on a journey from Durban to the Transvaal

1 inferior, *adj*: 低等
2 turban, *n*: 頭巾
3 insult, *v*: 侮辱

border, he had a first class ticket. Still, he was ordered to ride in second class. When he refused, his luggage was thrown off the train and he was shoved[1] onto the platform. Gandhi had to spend the night in the cold station, shivering without his topcoat which was in his lost luggage.

Gandhi was deeply offended by the bad treatment of his Indian brothers in South Africa. He made up his mind he would do something about it. He remembered reading in the Bhagavad-Gita that a good man was a man of action, working for justice.

Gandhi helped Dada Abdulla win the lawsuit. By then, he was nearing the end of the year he planned to spend in South Africa. But, to help his fellow Indians, he decided to spend some additional[2] time there.

---

1 shove, *v*: 推
2 additional, *adj*: 額外

A bill[1] called the "Indian Franchise" was in the South African legislature[2]. It was meant to deprive[3] Indians of the right to vote. Gandhi believed the right to vote was a basic human right. He organized meetings of Indians to protest the law with petitions[4].

Most Indians had come to South Africa as indentured servants[5]. They had promised to work for a period of time in exchange for their ticket to South Africa. Now they were little more than slaves. The government wanted to take from them what little rights they had. The Indians lost the voting battle.

Gandhi believed that the Indians in South Africa were citizens of the British Empire. He thought that they deserved equality[6] under the law. It was clear that Gandhi had a lot of work to do in South Africa. It seemed that he would not be returning home soon.

---

1   bill, *n*: 法案

2   legislature, *n*: 立法機關

3   deprive, *v*: 剝奪

4   petition, *n*: 請願書

5   indentured servant: 契約 僕人

6   equality, *n*: 平等

The Boer War 波耳戰爭

After three years in South Africa, Gandhi had become a successful lawyer with a good income. He was also a respected leader in the Indian community. He published a pamphlet[1] titled, "The Grievances of the British Indians in South Africa, an Appeal to the Indian Public." The pamphlet had a green cover. It soon became known as the "Green Book".

In 1896 Gandhi returned to India for a five-month visit with his family. He

---

1 pamphlet: 小冊子

decided that when he returned to South Africa, he would bring his wife and sons with him. Kasturba feared the move to South Africa. She could only speak the Gujarati language. She dreaded[1] being in a place where everyone around her spoke English or another foreign language. She was not sure she could survive such an unfamiliar place. She was also nervous about dealing with all the Muslim friends her husband had made.

Kasturba was a quiet, shy woman who took great comfort in family and friends she knew for a long time. But in the end, Gandhi convinced[2] his wife to move to South Africa. In all the disagreements between Mohandas and Kasturba Gandhi, he always won.

When Kasturba Gandhi arrived in South Africa, she had to give up her

---

1   dread, *v*: 害怕
2   convince, *v*: 説服

comfortable traditional clothing—the loose fitting dhoti*[1] and sandals. Now she would have to wear more modern clothing and hard leather shoes.

The Gandhi family moved to South Africa in 1897. Their third son, Ramdas, was born there. During Gandhi's absence from South Africa, the "Green Book" had become famous.

Although the Indian people loved the pamphlet, the Europeans hated it. Gandhi was attacked by mobs[2] of Europeans on the street. He was struck by rocks, mud, and garbage. He was cut in the neck before he was rescued from the mob.

There was a lot of tension in South Africa between the British and the Dutch. In 1899 full scale war broke out. It was called the Boer War*. Since Gandhi was a British citizen, he felt he

*Cultural Note

dhoti: 纏腰布，印度傳統男性服飾。用一塊白布從腰部圍起，穿過跨下再綁在腰部即可。

Boer War: 波耳戰爭。1899-1902 年間，因為川斯瓦共和國的普勒托利亞和瓦爾河間發現了金礦，使英國與川斯瓦共和國的波耳人間起了很大衝突。最後結果是南非共和國成立，並退出大英國協。

---

1   dhoti, *n*: 纏腰布
2   mob, *n*: 烏合之眾

had to side with the British. Gandhi did not believe in war. But he volunteered to form an ambulance corps[1] to help the British wounded.

Gandhi and other volunteers[2] carried wounded soldiers off the battlefield. The ambulance corps that Gandhi led consisted of African and Indian born Hindus, Muslims, and Christians. Gandhi hoped the good work done by the volunteers would impress the British. He hoped the British would grant more civil rights to Indians. Gandhi and thirty-eight members of the corps were awarded the South African War Medal for courage.

The Boer War ended with the British victory. The Union of South Africa was then established. South Africa withdrew from the British Commonwealth. It was ruled by Dutch politicians.

1　corps, *n*: 隊伍
2　volunteer, *n*: 志願者

Kasturba Gandhi had her fourth and last child, Devdas, in 1900. Her husband served as a midwife[1]. The Gandhis lived in a villa on the beach. Mohandas Gandhi ruled the family. He did not want a European education for his sons. Instead, he taught them himself. Gandhi was a stern father. His sons respected rather than loved him. Gandhi himself had a stern father. He was carrying on the tradition.

Gandhi forced his family to live a very simple life without luxuries[2]. They washed their own clothing. Gandhi cut his own hair. His friends sometimes said that his hair looked like a rat had chewed on it. Gandhi also made his wife get rid of her jewels, which were very special to her.

The worst sacrifice[3] for Kasturba Gandhi was having to empty the

---

1 midwife, *n*: 助产士

2 luxury, *n*: 奢侈品

3 sacrifice, *v*: 犠牲

chamber pots herself. In India, the untouchables did this work for her and all higher caste Indians. Now that this job fell to Kasturba, she felt humiliated[1]. She obeyed her husband but shed bitter tears.

In 1901 son Manilal became very ill with typhoid fever[2], which turned into pneumonia[3]. The doctor prescribed chicken broth and eggs for the child. But Gandhi's firm belief in vegetarianism forbade this. Gandhi treated Manilal himself. He gave his son many hot baths and had him drink orange juice and diluted milk. Gandhi remained at the boy's side for forty days. Manilal finally recovered. Gandhi called it a blessing from God for his own faithfulness to his principles.

---

1 humiliate, v: 羞辱
2 typhoid fever: 傷寒
3 pneumonia, n: 肺炎

Arrested 被捕

Gandhi bought eighty acres of fertile soil in South Africa. He founded[1] a community called Phoenix. It became the headquarters for Indian politics. Forty to fifty followers of Gandhi lived at Phoenix. There, they promoted[2] the simple way of life.

In 1905 there was a new law before the South African legislature called the Asiatic Law Agreement. The law was to prevent[3] further Asian immigration to South Africa. The whites did not want any more colored people.

---

1   found, *v*: 創辦

2   promote, *v*: 發揚

3   prevent, *v*: 預防

Under the new law, all Indians over the age of eight had to carry a registration card. Police could ask to see the card at any time. This was seen as a way to find and deport[1] illegal immigrants. Gandhi bitterly opposed this law and vowed a campaign of resistance called "Truth Force".

Hundreds and then thousands of Indians carried picket signs and marched in front of government offices. They protested what they called the "Black Law". Gandhi publicly announced that he would not register.

In January 1908 he was arrested for failing to register. He was taken before a judge. Gandhi was convicted[2] and sentenced[3] to two months in jail. This would be the first of many jail sentences Gandhi served while fighting for justice.

Gandhi eventually worked out a

---

1   deport, *v*: 驅逐出境

2   convict, *v*: 判為有罪

3   sentence, *v*: 判刑

compromise[1] with the government to make registration voluntary. He was on his way to register voluntarily when he was attacked by a Hindu. The Hindu man believed that Gandhi had given in on the issue. Gandhi was struck in the head with a stone, but he was not seriously hurt.

Harilal, Gandhi's eldest son, was unhappy with his father's strictness. Home schooled, Harilal longed for a formal education. When Harilal married a local girl his father opposed the marriage.

Then, Gandhi pushed his son into the battle for civil rights in South Africa. Harilal Gandhi was arrested. His wife and young son were left alone while he was in prison. Harilal blamed his father for the misfortune.

---

1 compromise, *v*: 妥協

Gandhi could clearly see how the Indians in South Africa were abused. But, he could not see how the black majority was even more cruelly treated. He briefly assisted the Zulus during one of their uprisings. He carried the Zulu[*1] wounded off the battlefield. But otherwise, he did not get involved in the victimization[2] of blacks.

In October 1908 Gandhi was again arrested for failing to carry his registration card. He was sentenced to two months at hard labor. Later, he got three months at hard labor.

He spent nine hours a day polishing the asphalt floor and iron door of his cell. By the time he was released in May 1909, his fame had spread beyond South Africa and India to the world. His battle for Indian rights for South Africa had captured the attention of the world press.

1   Zulu: 祖魯族
2   victimization, *n*: 犧牲

Gandhi traveled to London to explain his struggle. He published a pamphlet called "Home Rule". It asked Great Britain to grant independence[1] to India. He also asked the Indian people to return to their traditional ways. Harilal was now in full rebellion[2] against his father. He left South Africa for India. Now twenty-three, he desperately wanted the high school education he had been denied. He enrolled in an Indian high school.

The breach[3] between Harilal and his father was now so deep it would never be healed.

---

1   independence, *n*: 獨立
2   rebellion, *n*: 反抗
3   breach, *n*: 裂痕

Pleading for the rights of the people
為人民爭取權益

In March 1913 the South African government made all non-Christian marriages null and void[1]. Gandhi and other civil rights leaders reversed this quickly.

In June 1914 Gandhi made an agreement with the government which was a freedom charter for Indians. The Black Act was abolished[2], and all civil rights for Indians were returned to them. Gandhi called this a victory for his methods of peaceful resistance. In

---

1   null and void: 無效
2   abolish, *v*: 廢除

July 1914 Gandhi and his family returned to India.

At this time, World War I was breaking out. Germany, Austria, Hungary, and their allies were fighting against Great Britain, France, Russia, and their allies. At the time, Great Britain still ruled India along with some Indian princes.

Gandhi continued to oppose all war. Once again, he formed another ambulance corps to assist the wounded. Gandhi also asked Britain for home rule for India. He demanded an end to the untouchable class and equality for women.

There was one specific way in which women suffered greatly. That was the tradition that if a man died his wife was expected to jump onto the funeral pyre[1] to die as well.

---

1 pyre, *n*: 火葬柴堆

Gandhi built a community of followers at Sabarmati. He invited the untouchables to join. There were ten million untouchables in India. They were forbidden to use public roads or public wells. They had to live apart from other people.

Since the untouchables had little work, many had to scavenge[1] for food like animals. When Gandhi admitted the first untouchable family to Sabarmati, his wife was very upset.

Great Britain's Government of India Act of 1919 set up preliminary steps for eventual home rule for India. But the Rowlett Act of the same year established severe penalties for sedition[2]. Anything that disrupted daily life in the country could be called sedition.

Gandhi opposed the Rowlett Act. He called a hartal[3], or an Indian day of

---

1   scavenge, *v*: 在垃圾中覓食
2   sedition, *n*: 叛亂
3   hartal, *n*: 印度的罷工

mourning. All businesses were closed and there were massive protest demonstrations. Gandhi also fasted. The hartal spread throughout the country. It gave the Indian people a sense of new power. The hartal brought life to a standstill[1] in India.

In the City of Amritsar, the hartal turned violent. Two Englishmen were killed by an Indian mob. British General E. H. Dyer was sent in to restore order. He banned all further demonstrations in the city.

When ten to twenty thousand Indians gathered for a peaceful demonstration, Dyer ordered his troops to fire into the crowd. Gunfire rained on terrified people running for their lives. On that day, at least 379 died and hundreds were injured. Gandhi joined the rest of India in outrage against the atrocity[2].

---

1   standstill, *n*: 停滯不前
2   atrocity, *n*: 暴行

Principles of peaceful resistance
和平抵抗原則

In 1920, Gandhi joined the Indian Home Rule League. He became its first president. He now worked tirelessly for India's independence.

Everything in Gandhi helped make him a powerful leader in India. He had courage, vitality[1], and good humor. Although he was fiercely devoted to his cause, a smile would appear often on his toothless mouth. He was selfless, working always for the people.

---

1   vitality, *n*: 活力

The frail little man in the white dhoti, his wraparound garment[1], became a beloved symbol of peace and simplicity. Gandhi became the greatest hope the people had. He was Mahatma (Great Lord) Gandhi.

Gandhi toured India in steaming hot weather. He talked to crowds of one hundred thousand people or more during a seven month period. He ate three meals a day. The meals consisted of sixteen ounces of goat's milk, three slices of toast, two oranges, and a handful of grapes or raisins.

He preached[2] the simple, traditional way of life. He spun[3] cotton himself several hours each day. In the community of Sabarmati, cotton was planted. Only homespun clothing was worn. Gandhi prayed daily, chanting, "Rama, Rama, Rama" ("God, God, God").

---

1 garment, *n*: 服裝
2 preach, *v*: 講道
3 spin, *v*: 紡織

Gandhi wrote articles critical of British rule. He accused the British of shaking their "gory claws" into the face of India.

The British in India used Muslim volunteers in their army. Unlike the Hindus, the Muslims had no problem with military service.

Gandhi knew if he was to be successful in freeing India, he had to win the support of Muslims too. He wanted the Hindus and Muslims to work together as brothers. Gandhi designed a flag for independent India. It has three colors, red for Hindus, green for Muslims, and white for purity.

On February 5, 1921, a large demonstration for Indian independence at Chauri Chaura turned violent. The police clashed with the marchers and opened fire. When the police ran out of ammunition[1], the enraged crowd attacked them. They murdered some of the policemen. This horrified Gandhi.

On March 22, 1922, Gandhi was arrested for sedition. He was convicted and sentenced to six years in prison. Many Indians wept as the smiling Gandhi was led off to prison. He believed that every time he went to prison, he was bringing the day of Indian independence closer.

Gandhi was content[2] in prison. He arose at four in the morning to pray and meditate[3] for six hours. He read books and wrote letters. He spent hours spinning thread. But he did not serve the whole sentence. When he became sick with appendicitis[4], he was freed.

Much to Gandhi's sorrow, increasing violence between Hindus and Muslims

---

1   ammunition, *n*: 彈藥
2   content, *adj*: 滿足
3   meditate, *vt* & *vi*: 冥想
4   appendicitis, *n*: 盲腸炎

broke out. Gandhi began a twenty-one day fast for an end to the violence. On the twenty-first day, Hindus and Muslims came together to pray. Gandhi ended his fast.

In 1925 Gandhi again toured India to spread his ideas. Some Indians believed he was the reincarnation[1] of God. There were claims that he cured the sick. But Gandhi rejected all this. He said he was only a man and his power was just the power of persuasion[2].

Gandhi opposed child marriages, Urging[3] no woman under the age of twenty-one to be married. He was especially upset at the many child widows in India. Young girls were often married to older men and when the men died, the girls could not marry again.

---

1   reincarnation, *n*: 轉世
2   persuasion, *n*: 勸服
3   urge, *v*: 極力主張

At this time in India, there were more than eleven thousand widows[1] under the age of five. Eighty-five thousand widows were between five and ten. Altogether, almost four hundred thousand Indian girls under the age of fifteen were widows. Gandhi demanded that these girls be allowed to remarry.

In his struggle to improve the status of the untouchables, Gandhi gave them a new name: Harijans, which means children of God.

Gandhi believed India would become independent when it was spiritually[2] ready. He encouraged virtuous[3] living among the Indian people. He led discussions with Great Britain. Talks between Gandhi and other Indian leaders and the British fell apart in 1931. Again, Gandhi was arrested for his political activities.

---

1 widow, *n*: 寡婦
2 spiritually, *adv*: 精神上
3 virtuous, *adj*: 合乎道德

Gandhi fasted in prison. As he lay in the shade of a mango tree in the prison yard, he grew very weak. The British, afraid he would die in their hands, freed him.

As Gandhi struggled for his goals, the personal tragedy of his relationship with his son, Harilal grew worse. Harilal was often drunk. He wrote mean letters to his father accusing him of being abusive.[1] In 1936 Harilal became a Muslim. Gandhi was deeply saddened.

In the 1930s the world was again moving toward a terrible war. Germany, under Adolf Hitler, was grabbing territory in Europe. Italy, under Benito Mussolini, attacked Ethiopia in Africa. Japan had invaded[2] China.

These three countries, Germany, Italy, and Japan formed a dangerous alliance

---

1   abusive, *adj*: 虐待
2   invade, *v*: 入侵

called the Axis. The Axis* threatened the peace of the world. Gandhi clung to his peaceful principles. Even in the face of such massive evil as Adolf Hitler, Gandhi believed that a peaceful approach would work.

Gandhi said that if a country was attacked by the Axis powers, it should not fight back. Rather, people should not cooperate[1] with the invaders. He believed with total peaceful resistance, the invaders would be stopped. Many people thought Gandhi was living in a dream world.

Gandhi insisted that even if an aggressor like Hitler took over a country, he could occupy[2] the land, but he could not conquer[3] the minds, hearts, and souls of the people. In this way, Hitler would fail in the end. Gandhi's pacifist[4] attitude in the face of Axis aggression around the world made the

---

1　cooperate, *vi*: 合作

2　occupy, *vi*: 佔領

3　conquer, *v*: 征服

4　pacifist, *n*: 和平主義者

British angry. They wanted active participation of India in the fight against the Axis, and Gandhi was preaching peace. The British once again arrested Gandhi in 1942, along with his wife, Kasturba.

Kasturba Gandhi
甘地的妻子卡絲托芭‧甘地

C H A P T E R 10

Independence and partition
獨立與分裂

Kasturba Gandhi had a weak heart. While she was in prison, she experienced shortness of breath. She could no longer sleep lying down. Instead she sat up at night with her head resting on a table. She felt that she would soon die. She asked that her sons come. She wanted to see them for the last time.

Manilal Gandhi was in South Africa, and he could not come. The other three sons arrived at their mother's bedside. Harilal was drunk when he came. He was not allowed to see his mother until he was sober[1]. When he was able to see her, Kasturba was overcome with joy.

In December 1943 Kasturba got pneumonia[2]. Her sons asked that she be given penicillin[3]. But Gandhi insisted on treating her by natural means, with honey and water. On February 22, 1944, Kasturba died with her head resting in her husband's lap. They had been married for sixty-two years. Gandhi felt that his wife had become a part of himself. Now, part of him had died.

At her funeral, Hindus, Muslims, and Christians prayed, sang hymns, and wept together. Kasturba's body was cremated[4] in a funeral pyre according to Hindu tradition. Her ashes were buried on the prison grounds.

---

1   sober, *adj*: 清醒
2   pneumonia, *n*: 肺炎
3   penicillin, *n*: 盤尼西林
4   cremate, *vt*: 火葬

Soon after Kasturba's death, Gandhi became ill with malaria[1]. The British freed him. They were always afraid to have him die while he was in their custody[2]. Gandhi walked from the prison on May 6, 1944. This was his last prison stay. He had spent two thousand and eighty-nine days in Indian prisons and two hundred and forty-nine days in South African prisons.

Gandhi now focused all his attention on uniting Hindus and Muslims and gaining independence for India. But, he faced terrible odds. The Muslims in India wanted the country to be divided. They wanted one part to be given to them and the other part to the Hindus. Gandhi wanted one united country with all religions treating one another as brothers.

---

1   malaria, *n*: 瘧疾
2   custody, *n*: 監禁

In 1946 violence between the Hindus and Muslims became so terrible that thousands died. Men, women, and children died on both sides. Gandhi was horrified and heartbroken. He traveled on foot across India pleading[1] for peace. He begged the Hindus and the Muslims to give up their hatred and live together. But, the violence continued.

Finally on August 15, 1947, India was divided into two countries, Pakistan for the Muslims and India for the Hindus. This caused there to be millions of Hindu and Muslim refugees. The Muslim refugees[2] fled into Pakistan. Hindus in Pakistan fled into India. India and Pakistan were now independent.

The violence continued even after the countries separated. On January 13, 1948, Gandhi began his final fast for an

---

1   plead, *v*: 懇求
2   refugee, *n*: 難民

end to violence. Gandhi was living in Birla House. During the fast, he lay in a crouched position with his knees pulled up toward his stomach. He was losing two pounds a day. His eyes were closed as if in sleep.

When he spoke to those who came to support him, his voice was weak. He asked all Indians to purify themselves and put an end once and for all to violence. On the morning of January 18, a pledge was drafted by Hindus, Muslims, and others, promising tolerance[1] for one another. Overcome with joy, Gandhi ended his fast.

Not all Hindus were pleased with Gandhi's philosophy. Some blamed him for the fact that now India had been separated.

Some traditional Hindus clung to[2] the belief that the untouchables had to be

---

1   tolerance, *n*: 寬容
2   cling to: 堅持

maintained in a lower position. They resented Gandhi's efforts to free the untouchables from their burdens. From among these angry people came thirty-five-year-old Nathuram Godse, a newspaper editor. He began to plot against Gandhi.

On January 25, 1948, Gandhi arrived at a prayer meeting in good spirits. He had been told that tolerance was growing among Hindus and Muslims. It was a cold day. Gandhi asked that the people who came to pray be given straw mats to sit on since the ground was damp.

Nathuram Godse was in the front row of the people who had come to see Gandhi. He had a pistol[1] in his pocket. Most of the people bowed respectfully when Gandhi appeared. Godse did the same. Gandhi touched his palms

---

1   pistol, *n*: 手槍

together. He smiled and blessed the people who had gathered.

Suddenly Godse pushed forward. He fired three shots at Gandhi from his small automatic pistol. The first bullet struck Gandhi's stomach and came out his back. Gandhi remained standing. The second bullet tore through the center of his body, also going out the back. His white garment ran red with blood. Gandhi's face turned white. The third shot entered his lung.

"Hey Rama!" (Oh God!) Gandhi cried. His glasses fell off. The sandals dropped from his feet as he slipped to the ground. As Gandhi was carried to Birla House, Godse was seized by the crowd.

Gandhi still had a pulse[1] when he was laid down. But, when the doctors

---

1 pulse, *n*: 脉搏

arrived, there was nothing they could do. Gandhi's face was peaceful in death as Hindu prayers were chanted around his body.

Gandhi's body was washed and thousands prayed and wept as he was carried to Jumna where he was laid on a funeral pyre. A million people shouted "long live Mahatma Gandhi" as the fire consumed his body.

As the pyre burned, a frail man, his body racked with tuberculosis[1], stood at the edge of the crowd. It was Gandhi's son, Harilal. He came to pay his respects. Gandhi's ashes were cast into the holy Ganges River*.

From all over the world came words of praise for the peaceful little man who brought independence to India. Gandhi was the man who taught the world that revolutions could be won by

*Cultural Note

Ganges River: 恆河，印度的聖河。印度人相信恆河的水可以洗去罪惡，人死後若將骨灰灑進恆河，能得到更好的來生。

1   tuberculosis, *n*: 結核病

peaceful resistance. Gandhi fought his battles without hatred. He preached kindness and tolerance to all.

Martin Luther King Jr. was the Baptist preacher[1] who led the civil rights movement in America in the 1950s and 1960s. He embraced Gandhi's principles of nonviolence, even in the face of brutal attacks. Just as Gandhi refused to stoop[2] to hatred as he struggled to free India, King clung to nonviolence in his successful crusade to end discrimination in the United States.

General Douglas MacArthur, famous military leader of World War II, commented on Mahatma Gandhi's death. He said that if civilization itself is to survive, all mankind must eventually accept Gandhi's philosophy.

Mahatma Gandhi, by his life and death, witnessed to peace.

---

1   preacher, *n*: 牧師
2   stoop, *v*: 屈服

Exercises 練習

1. Vocabulary 詞彙

1.1 Syllables 音節

按音節提示填入正確詞彙。請見示範。

1. Three-syllable word that means "to give up something valuable"
   <u>sacrifice</u>
2. Two-syllable word that means "a piece of cloth that is worn on the head" _____
3. Three-syllable word that means "having many good qualities" ____
4. One-syllable word that means "to not eat in protest" _____
5. Three-syllable word that means "an agreement between two parties" _____
6. Two-syllable word that means "to find guilty of an act" _____

1.2 Label groups 分類標示

以下每題目均含同類詞彙，請加一個同類詞語，並用英語寫出類別。請見示範。

1. Muslims   Hindus   Jews   <u>Christians; they are all religions.</u>
2. Harilal   Ramdas   Devdas _____
3. March   fast   boycott _____
4. India   China   Vietnam _____
5. scholars   warriors   traders _____
6. France   Great Britain   Germany _____

2. Understanding 理解

2.1 Analogies 比擬

先看表格內右欄的比擬，在左欄寫出每個比擬關係的類型，填入適當詞語完成右欄。請見示範。

Type of analogies	Analogies
1. synonyms	1. attorney : lawyer :: professor : teacher
	2. Gandhi : pacifist leader :: Franklin Roosevelt : _____
	3. India : New Delhi :: _____ : Washington, D.C.
	4. war : _____ :: large : small
	5. Hinduism : religion :: Hindi :

Part 2

Cesar Chavez
凱薩・查維斯

Chavez's growth
查維斯的成長

*Cultural Note

migrant workers: 外來勞工。墨西哥一直是美國廉價勞工市場的主要來源，尤其是農業。十九世紀中期，美國落實布拉塞洛計劃，讓墨西哥的工人可以臨時合約制來美國工作。

On November 20, 1960, there was a show on CBS called Harvest of Shame. It was about the migrant workers* who harvest America's food. The show called attention to the fact that migrant[1] farm workers were poverty-stricken[2] and neglected. They lived in bad housing. They lacked decent pay and health insurance. Often, migrant workers were sprayed with deadly chemicals as they worked in the fields.

1　migrant, *n*: 移民
2　poverty-stricken, *adj*: 很窮

Cesar Chavez was a Mexican American farm worker. He was the first person to make changes in the lives of farm workers. Cesar did not have much education or money. Powerful people worked against him. But he managed to help the migrant workers win more economic safety and dignity. He did this by leading a nonviolent revolution.

Cesar Estrada Chavez was born on March 31, 1927, in Yuma, Arizona. He was the second child of Juana and Librado Chavez. Librado Chavez was thirty-eight when he married Juana Estrada. Librado was working on his father's farm as a rancher[1] at the time.

The Chavez's ranch was in the North Gila Valley in the Arizona desert. Librado worked on the ranch. He also ran three small businesses: a garage, a pool hall, and a candy store.

---

1   rancher, *n*: 大農場主

Librado's father was a migrant worker from Mexico before he got the ranch in Arizona. The family grew sweet Malaga grapes, melons, squash, beans, lettuce, tomatoes, and hot peppers. They also raised chickens, milk cows, and sheep.

Cesar and his younger brother, Richard, were good friends. They both loved to play pool in their free time. Their mother was very religious. She taught them to help the poor.

The Chavez family was not rich. But they had a home and enough to eat. When migrant workers passed through, the Chavez family always tried to help them. Migrant workers often shared the evening meal with the Chavez family.

Juana Chavez also taught her children to avoid fighting. She told them that it always takes two people to start a fight.

She said that there is always a better way to solve problems. Cesar never forgot this lesson.

Cesar and his brothers and sisters had a good life when they were kids. They had many chores[1], but there was also time for fun. The children swam and fished in the river and flew kites. On Sundays, the whole family climbed into the old family Studebaker and went to the Catholic church in Yuma.

When Cesar was two-years-old, the Great Depression* began in the United States. It began when the stock market crashed in 1929. The value of stocks fell quickly. Many people lost their jobs.

People also lost their houses and farms. Many Americans did not have any food. It took time for the hard times to reach everyone. In 1937 hard times came to the Chavez family.

the Great Depression：美國經濟大蕭條，指 1929 年至 1933 年之間全球性的經濟大衰退。

---

1   chore, *n*: 農莊雜務

There was a drought[1] and economic depression in Arizona. Very little water ran down the Colorado River. This meant that irrigation ditches ran dry.

Land that once grew healthy crops, now was dry and cracked. People had no crops to sell. The Chavez family could not pay their property taxes.

Librado Chavez went to Yuma and asked for a loan at the bank. The bank would not give him a loan, and he lost all three of his businesses. The Chavez farm was sold at a public auction. Librado, Juana, and their children had to pack all of their things into the Studebaker and leave their home.

The Chavez family had always felt sorry for the homeless migrant workers who went from one field to the next searching for work. Now, they were part of that sad group.

---

1 drought, *n*: 乾旱

CHAPTER 2

Father's influence 父親影響

The Chavez family drove west to California. They got to the Imperial Valley and stopped in a migrant camp in Brawley. Cesar saw rows of rundown[1] shacks where the migrants lived. Cesar was ten years old, and he had never seen such a difficult place to live.

The migrant workers had to pay two dollars a night to live in one of the shacks. Since the Chavez family had no money, they had to keep going. They pulled off[2] the road when it got dark and slept in the Studebaker.

---

1   rundown, *adj*: 破舊
2   pull off: 靠邊

The next day the Chavez family found a job picking grapes. They were told that they would be paid at the end of the week. The whole family worked all week. But they were not paid as they were promised. There was nothing they could do. Migrant workers had to take whatever was done to them.

They could not afford to pay rent for a migrant shack. Many times, Cesar and his family lived under bridges. When they could not find work, the children gathered mustard greens from the roadside. That was all they had to eat.

Cesar and his brother, Richard, worked with their parents in the fields. Sometimes they found ways to earn extra money, too. One time, the boys collected tinfoil[1] from cigarette, candy, and gum wrappers[2]. They made a huge ball with the tinfoil. They sold the ball to a junk dealer. They were able to buy

---

1   tinfoil, *n*: 錫紙

2   wrapper, *n*: 包裝紙

two sweatshirts and a pair of tennis shoes with the money.

Later, someone told Cesar and his family that pea pickers were needed in Atascadero, California. When they got there, all the fields were already picked. There was no work for them. They moved to Gonzales and lived in a small room above a bar. They worked in the pea fields nearby. In three hours of work, the whole family could make only twenty cents.

When there was less farming work, the Chavez children went to any school that was close by. Cesar went to thirty or forty schools during his childhood. The teachers often thought the migrant children were a problem.

Since the children spent very little time in school, they were always behind in class. The migrant children spoke

Spanish at home. But they were not allowed to speak Spanish in school.

Cesar was often hit with a ruler across his knuckles for speaking Spanish. In some classrooms, the Mexican American children were separated from the other children. This was very difficult for them.

The Chavez family always went to church in Yuma. Now, they did not have a church. Sometimes, a priest would come to the migrant camps on Sunday. He would stand in the back of his pickup truck and say Mass. Cesar would often help the priest during Mass. Often, the priest would pass out[1] clothing, food, and toys for the children. The people were always in need of these things.

In California, conditions for the grape pickers were very bad. They worked all

---

1   pass out: 分發

day in the hot sun. If they wanted a drink of water, they had to pay a nickel for it.

One night, Cesar's father met with other grape pickers to talk about the bad conditions. They decided to demand better pay and working conditions. If things did not get better, they would go on strike[1]. Cesar was only thirteen, but he always listened to the men talking.

Cesar's father went to the owner of the vineyard. He told him that the men would strike if conditions did not get better. The owner said that Librado Chavez was a Communist who wanted to start a revolution. At that time, being called a Communist was very bad.

The owner would not change the conditions or the pay. The workers went on strike. They hoped the owner would worry that his grapes would rot[2] on the

---

1   on strike: 罷工
2   rot, v: 腐爛

vine. They wanted him to agree to make changes.

The workers marched around the vineyard in a picket line*. The owner brought in new workers to pick his grapes. He hired people called braceros[1]. Braceros were workers from Mexico. They were allowed to come to the United States to do work that local people would not do.

The braceros all had very poor families in Mexico. They were desperate for work. They sent their money home to their parents, wives, and children.

The braceros did the work, so the strike was broken. There was no reason for the migrant workers to keep picketing. Librado Chavez and the other workers were fired.

---

1 bracero, *n*: 墨西哥短期合同工

The Chavez family went to San Jose. They lived in a barrio called Sal si Puedes, which means "get out if you can". It was a poor neighborhood with a lot of crime.

Farmers were paying one and a half cents a pound for picked cherries. After the cherry harvest was over, there was the apricot harvest. Once the apricots were picked, they were pitted and cut in half. They then were laid on drying tables in the sun. The Chavez family made thirty cents a day picking apricots.

Later, in Oxnard, California, Cesar and his family harvested walnuts. Cesar and Richard slept outside in the open. The younger children slept in an eight-foot-long tent. In the winter, cold winds blew in from the ocean. The children's shoes rotted from the cold.

C H A P T E R **3**

Witness discrimination against Mexican Americans 目擊美籍墨西哥人被歧視

In 1942 Librado Chavez was injured in a car accident. He could not work for awhile. Cesar was fifteen-years-old. He finished seventh grade, but he now had to quit school. He had to earn money for the family. Cesar traveled as a migrant worker by himself.

He went to fields around the state, following the crops. He worked in fields of lettuce and sugar beets. Since he had to use a short handled hoe, he was always bent over. Cesar had constant backaches. Then, he followed the onion planting season. Again, he had to bend over all day. He dug his fingers into the ground and planted the onion seedlings.

World War II had started. All over America, young men were joining the military. In 1944 seventeen-year-old Cesar Chavez signed up for the United States Navy. He became a deck hand[1] on a ship.

By this time, Librado Chavez could work again. There were many men off fighting in the war, so it was easier for the Chavez family to get farm work. The pay improved as well.

The Chavez family was living in Delano at that time. Cesar Chavez started to notice a lot of discrimination[2] against Mexicans. Many restaurants would not serve Mexicans.

---

1   deck hand: 甲板水手
2   discrimination, *n*: 歧視

One time, Chavez walked into a movie theater. He sat down in the section for white people. One of the people who worked at the theater told him to go to the section for African Americans, Filipinos, and Mexicans. Chavez would not move, so the police were called. The police officer gave Chavez a strong warning for his actions.

Cesar met Helen Fabela at an ice cream store in Delano. They liked each other very much. In 1946 Cesar left the navy. Then, he and Helen began to date[1] seriously.

Cesar was five feet six inches tall, and he weighed 135 pounds. He looked older than he was because of so many years of hard work. He had little education, so he could only get farm work. He worked hard and started to save money for his marriage.

---

1   date, *v*: 約會

In 1948 Cesar Chavez married Helen Fabela. On their honeymoon, they visited all of the missions of California. Then, they went back to Delano. They rented a one-room shack with no electricity and no running water. The only heat came from a small camping stove. The couple did not have a car, so they had to ask for rides everywhere.

Cesar and Helen Chavez picked grapes and lettuce in the summer. In the winter, they picked cotton. Soon, Helen was pregnant with their first baby. Only Cesar worked in the fields then.

On February 20, 1949, Fernando was born. Cesar Chavez was making more money, and in 1950, their daughter Sylvia was born. Next, came Linda in 1951.

Chavez and his brother, Richard, rented a small farm in Greenfield,

California. There, they tried to grow strawberries. The two men remembered that their father and grandfather farmed their own land in Arizona. They wanted that better life for their families. But the strawberry farm did not work out.[1] Chavez went back to picking beans for a dollar to a dollar and a half per hour. Two more children were born, Eloise in 1952 and Ana in 1953.

The Chavez family returned to San Jose. There, Cesar met Father Donald McDonnell, who had a strong impact on his life. Cesar and the priest talked about farm work and the problems of the migrants. Because of Father McDonnell, Chavez began to read books about St. Francis of Assisi, the gentle saint.

He also read about Mahatma Gandhi*. Gandhi was a Hindu man who helped

*Cultural Note

Mahatma Gandhi：穆罕達默・甘地。通過 "非暴力" 的手法，帶領印度邁向獨立，脫離英國的殖民統治。

---

1 work out: 成功

bring independence to India. Chavez found the same nonviolent message in these books that his mother taught him. Chavez was very interested to learn how much people could do using peaceful ways.

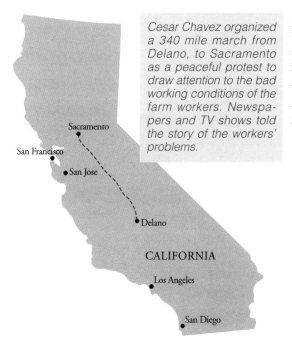

Cesar Chavez organized a 340 mile march from Delano, to Sacramento as a peaceful protest to draw attention to the bad working conditions of the farm workers. Newspapers and TV shows told the story of the workers' problems.

凱薩查維斯發起340英里的和平示威，由德拉諾遊行到山克拉門都，希望社會關注農業工人的惡劣工作環境。電視及報章亦有報導他們的苦況。

C H A P T E R 4

Organising a march 組織農工遊行

Cesar Chavez then met a man who changed his life. Fred Ross was an Anglo social worker. He worked for President Franklin Roosevelt's Farm Security Administration. His job was to organize food distribution, like beans and flour, to poor people.

Ross wanted to do more. He wanted to help people rise from poverty. He wanted to help the poor to help themselves. But he was working in the

Mexican American neighbourhoods in San Jose. Ross needed a strong, smart Mexican leader to bring his program to the people.

Ross started the Community Service Organization (CSO). He started to search for a Mexican leader who could help him talk to the people. Then, he met Cesar Chavez. He asked Chavez if he could get a group of his friends together at his house. Ross wanted to come speak to them about the CSO. Chavez agreed, but he and his friends were very suspicious of Ross.

Often, Anglo men came into the barrio with ideas that ended up being worthless. When Ross got up to speak, many complained and were not interested. But slowly, the men began to like Ross's message. The CSO seemed to be a good thing. They were trying to register Mexican American voters. When the elections came, the Mexican Americans would have some say in who was elected. An election was coming in 1952. The CSO hoped the people elected would be interested in the needs of the poor.

Ross hired Cesar Chavez as a recruiter[1] for the CSO. Chavez went from house to house in the neighborhood registering his neighbors. With Chavez's help, six thousand new voters were registered.

Now, Ross asked Chavez to take on more responsibility. He wanted him to be an organizer. He asked Chavez to lead meetings. Chavez was only twenty-five and he was very nervous about getting up in front of a group of people and telling them what needed to be done. Some of them were old enough to be his parents.

---

1 recruiter, *n*: 招聘人員

Chavez held back[1] his fear and gave his first CSO meeting in Oakland, California. Chavez was surprised to find that the crowd was very interested. They showed him a lot of respect.

Cesar Chavez was now earning $58.00 a week as an organizer. He traveled all over California, from Bakersfield to Oxnard. He was recruiting people for CSO. In 1957 his son, Paul, was born. Then, in 1958 Anthony and Elizabeth were born. There were now eight children in the family.

One of the first problems that Cesar Chavez dealt with was the lack of farm jobs in Oxnard. Whenever farm workers were needed, the local farm workers were turned away. Instead, the farmers hired the braceros from Mexico. It was illegal to hire braceros if local workers were available, but the law was broken.

1　hold back: 抑制

On January 15, 1959, Chavez organized a protest march of 1,500 farm workers. The workers demanded they be given a chance to fill the jobs in Oxnard. The growers preferred braceros because no matter how bad the working conditions were, they never complained. They were afraid that they would be sent back to Mexico. If they were sent back, they could not help their families by sending money home. So, they would put up with the injustice in silence.

The U. S. Secretary of Labor, James Mitchell, came to Oxnard to talk to the local business people. Chavez organized a march of ten thousand people to get his attention. They marched behind the banner of Our Lady of Guadalupe*, a very sacred symbol for Mexican American people.

*Cultural Note

Our Lady of Guadalupe：瓜達盧佩聖母，是墨西哥的守護神。

The marchers sang hymns and carried signs demanding justice. The marchers had no police permit. But there were so many of them that the police did not even try to make arrests. It was a very peaceful demonstration.

After thirteen months of struggle, the Oxnard growers finally gave in and agreed to hire local farm workers. It was Cesar Chavez's first big labor victory. It had been a hard year. Chavez worked so hard that he lost twenty-five pounds off his already thin body. Chavez was now earning $150 a week plus expenses as a national CSO director. But he had a bigger dream. He wanted to form a union just for farm workers.

Launching the Farm Workers Labour Union 創辦農民工會

Cesar Chavez talked to the CSO directors about his farm union. Since they were not interested, he resigned. In 1962 Chavez had saved $1,200. With Helen's help and her family's support, he believed he could launch[1] the Farm Workers Labour Union.

Chavez drew a map of every town and migrant camp in the San Joaquin Valley. There were 86 in all. He planned to visit each one of them to recruit workers for

---

1   launch, *v*: 創辦

his union, the National Farm Workers Association (NFWA).

He set up headquarters in his garage. He loaded his Mercury station wagon with sign up sheets. He took his son, Anthony, on some of the trips because there was nobody to leave the boy with. Helen Chavez was working.

Sometimes, Chavez actually went from door to door and to gathering places where migrant workers could be found. Right away, he recruited a spirited young woman, Dolores Huerta. She deeply believed in the principles of justice. She had worked at the CSO with Chavez. She believed in his cause and became a strong force in the union.

Even the Chavez children were recruited to help in the early days. After school on Friday, they would pile into the Mercury. Their arms were full of leaflets that their mother had run off the night before on an old mimeograph[1] machine. The older children also helped earn money for the family. They went with their mother to the fields to pick cotton, walnuts, peas, and table grapes. This way, their father had time to organize the union.

Dolores Huerta signs up workers to join the union.
多洛雷絲・韋爾塔（Dolores Huerta）為工人登記加入工會。

---

1 mimeograph, *n*: 油印

By the fall of 1962, one thousand farm workers had joined the union. Chavez decided there were enough members to hold a convention in Fresno, California. In Fresno, the union flag was unveiled.

Chavez had put a lot of thought into the flag. He wanted it to be simple so that farm workers could easily copy it to make their own posters and flags. So, he chose the sacred Aztec* bird, the eagle, and drew it in straight lines. The black eagle was on a white circle and the rest of the flag was red. The black eagle was a symbol of the troubles the farm workers had endured. White stood for hope. Red was for the struggle for justice. The motto[1] of the union was "Viva la Causa" or long live the cause.

Union dues[2] were $3.50 a month. Benefits to the workers included a credit bank that would loan money at low interest. There was also a burial society

---

1   motto, *n*: 座右銘

2   dues, *n*: 會費

that would cover the funeral expenses of poor workers. Chavez also set up a co-operative grocery store and gas station that sold things at lower prices. Cesar Chavez's salary as union president was $35.00 a week, which included his wife's bookkeeping services.

Chavez also started a union newspaper, *El Malcriado**. El malcriado means "the brat", and the paper cried out against injustices. Cesar Chavez's first big challenge was with the grape growers of Delano, California. Grape workers there earned about a dollar an hour. Their average yearly income was $1,500.

At the time, the poverty level in the United States had been set at $3,000 a year for a family. On many grape ranches, there were no toilets in the fields. Workers had to pay for drinking water. Dangerous chemicals were

*Cultural Note

El Malcriado：（西班牙語）原意指頑童，是墨西哥革命期間其中一份民報的名字。查維斯其後亦發行另一份同名的報章，作為工人們的發聲工具，別具意義。

98

frequently sprayed[1] on the vineyards while workers were present. This created great risks to their health.

The AFL-CIO already had an agricultural union called the Agricultural Workers of California. They were fighting for the rights of Filipino workers. Filipino farm worker, Larry Itliong, was trying to organize his fellow Filipinos to get better working conditions.

He called a strike in September 1965. But the growers found some Mexican workers to break the strike. So, Itliong talked to Cesar Chavez. Chavez's union voted to join Itliong's cause. Then, Filipino and Mexican farm workers stood side by side.

On the first day of the strike, 1,200 workers walked out from the vineyard. They formed picket lines on the roads

---

1   spray, *v*: 噴

leading into the grape farm. Some growers turned to violence. They pointed shotguns at the strikers. They knocked some of them to the ground and set fire to their picket signs.

The growers roared down the dirt roads in trucks. They showered picketers with gravel and dirt. Some growers even intentionally shot fertilizer and insecticides from spraying machines at the strikers.

The police and sheriffs in the area usually sided with the growers. Although the farm union was nonviolent, their members were arrested for various reasons. Dolores Huerta was arrested twice in one week and charged with trespassing. Chavez and a Catholic priest flew over the vineyard in a private plane. When they landed, they were arrested and charged with violating the air space of the grower. Cesar Chavez insisted on complete nonviolence no matter what happened.

To keep the strikers going without their paychecks[1], Chavez raised money at rallies[2] around California. He appeared at the University of California, Berkeley. The college students donated generously. Help came from many different sources. One dairy donated a hundred dozen eggs a week. A meat packing plant gave forty pounds of hamburger each Saturday. Bakeries donated day-old[3] bread and rolls.

However, the grape strike was not succeeding. The farm workers needed another weapon. That weapon was a boycott of grapes.

---

1   paycheck, *n*: 薪水
2   rally, *n*: 集會
3   day-old: 隔夜

CHAPTER 6

The Grape Strike 罷買葡萄爭取權益

Cesar Chavez's farm workers picketed the docks where grapes were loaded for shipment to other countries. The UFW asked people all over California and the United States to stop buying grapes until the growers accepted the union's demands.

In 1965 Chavez focused attention on Schenley Industries, which had 3,350 acres of grapes in Delano. Chavez used a "divide and conquer"[1] strategy. He targeted one grower at a time. In December 1965 the AFL-CIO officially

---

1   divide and conquer: 分步解決

endorsed[1] the grape strike. It made a large donation to the workers' strike fund.

In March 1966 the United States Senate Subcommittee investigated the grape strike and held hearings[2] in Delano. Senator Robert Kennedy of New York was a member of the subcommittee. He was very sympathetic to Chavez. During the hearings, Chavez and Kennedy became close friends

At this time, a farm worker's march to Sacramento began. The marchers asked for passage of a law to guarantee fair farm labor wages. The group marched behind American and Mexican flags, the banner of Our Lady of Guadalupe, and the UFW eagle. They covered 21 miles the first day. Chavez's ankle was badly swollen. He had a large blister[3] on his foot. By the second day, Chavez's right leg was swollen to his knee. He had to ride in the station wagon.

---

1   endorse, *v*: 支援
2   hearing, *n*: 聽證會
3   blister, *n*: 水泡

As the march passed through towns and cities, the marchers were greeted by sympathizers playing guitars and accordions[1]. By the ninth day, Chavez could walk again with the help of a cane. The marchers were treated to lunch by the mayor of Fresno. In Stockton, five thousand people cheered them. At that time, Chavez received a phone call from Schenley Industries recognizing the union and agreeing to terms.

It was raining on Easter Sunday as the marchers got together in Sacramento. Chavez told the 10,000 who came to welcome the marchers that a historic agreement had been reached with Schenley Industries. With the exception of a pineapple workers contract made earlier, this was the first American farm workers contract in U. S. history.

---

1 accordion, *n*: 手風琴

The next target of the UFW was the DiGiorgio Corporation's 4,400 acre vineyard in Sierra Vista. DiGiorgio was well known for breaking strikes. They had broken them in the 1930s, 40s, and 60s. They had strong political influence in the state.

Now, DiGiorgio agreed to talk to the UFW and to hold elections among their farm workers. But the Teamsters* were also trying to recruit farm workers. The Teamsters was another union that represented workers in the area at the time. DiGiorgio was sure that the Teamsters would win. DiGiorgio wanted to work with the Teamsters because they thought they would get a better agreement from them.

*Cultural Note

Teamsters: 卡車司機工會是美國很有勢力的一個全國工會，其成員不只卡車司機，還有其他許多以體力勞動為主的工人。

Arrested 被捕

Cesar Chavez merged his United Farm workers with the AWOC. The new name for the union was United Farm Workers of California (UFWOC). The election began among the farm workers. They were asked to choose which union they wanted to represent them.

At the same time, DiGiorgio got a court order against Chavez for picketing. The Teamsters intimidated[1]

---

1 intimidate, *v*: 恐嚇

some of the farm workers to try to gain their votes. But, when the votes were counted, the UFWOC won by a wide margin[1].

Cesar with his wife, Helen, at his side, began negotiating with the grape growers for better wages and working conditions for the union members.
凱薩・查維斯及他的妻子海倫，就工會會員的工資及工作環境與葡萄種植者進行談判。

---

1 margin, *n*: 差數

In August 1967 Cesar Chavez began a fast[1] to affirm the nonviolent nature of his struggle. Some of the younger members of the UFW were getting impatient. They wanted more aggressive measures. But Chavez insisted on the way of peace.

The grape strike was now known all over America. Many people boycotted grapes as a matter of conscience[2]. If people did not see the emblem of the black eagle on a box of grapes, they refused to buy it. The eagle symbol meant that the grower had come to terms with the UFW union.

One by one, the grape growers were making deals with Chavez. On July 17, 1970, the big break came. Twenty-three growers were ready to negotiate. They grew almost half of all the grapes in California.

---

1   fast, *n*: 絕食
2   conscience, *n*: 良心

Negotiations were held at the Holiday Inn in Bakersfield. The growers agreed to hire union workers, protect the workers against pesticides, and raise wages to $1.80 an hour. The grape strike ended. It was a huge victory for Chavez and his union.

Now, Cesar Chavez turned his attention to another group of farm workers, the lettuce pickers of Salinas, California. The Teamsters were already making a lot of progress with the lettuce[1] workers. At the end of July 1970, Chavez held a large rally in Salinas. He argued that the Teamsters were not getting good contracts for the workers. The UFWOC could do better. Fights broke out between UFWOC workers and Teamsters.

In August 1970 Chavez called for a nationwide boycott of Chiquita

---

1 lettuce, *n*: 生菜

bananas, which were marketed by a large lettuce grower. The same day, the company asked for negotiations. Chavez was able to get good terms for the lettuce pickers. The Teamsters struck back, and UFWOC workers were threatened with baseball bats and chains. The windscreen[1] of their cars were broken.

Chavez was ordered by the court to end his lettuce boycott against the growers. But the growers would not agree to the terms of the negotiation, so he refused to end the boycott. He was arrested. At his December hearing, two thousand workers marched around the courthouse praying and carrying candles. Chavez was ordered to remain in jail until he agreed to end the lettuce boycott.

1　windscreen, *n*: 擋風玻璃，美 windshield

CHAPTER 8

Fasts to help his people 為民絕食

Cesar Chavez's farm workers made a makeshift[1] shrine[2] in a pickup truck across the street from the jail where Chavez was being held. Many famous civil rights leaders came to visit Chavez and to offer their support for his cause. Coretta Scott King came to pray with Chavez. She was the widow of Dr. Martin Luther King Jr.*, who was assassinated in 1968. Ethel Kennedy, widow of Senator Robert Kennedy, who was also assassinated in 1968, paid her respects to the jailed Chavez.

*Cultural Note

Martin Luther King Jr.: 馬丁・路德・金。黑人民權領袖,主張採用非暴力手段,於1964 獲得諾貝爾和平獎。

---

1 makeshift, *adj*: 臨時
2 shrine, *n*: 聖壇

Twenty days later, the California Supreme Court ordered the release of Chavez. They said he had the right to conduct the lettuce boycott as part of his free speech rights. But talks with the lettuce growers broke down. Although Chavez continued to fight to establish his union in the lettuce fields, the Teamsters were too strong. Cesar Chavez did not have the success in the lettuce fields that he had in the grape vineyards.

In 1972 anti-union forces in California got an issue on the ballot[1] that would ban the boycott and many other effective labor weapons. Proposition[2] 22 was widely promoted before the election. Chavez started a large campaign to defeat it. Proposition 22 went down to defeat 58 percent to 42 percent.

---

1   ballot, *n*: 投票
2   proposition, *n*: 提案

In May 1972 a similar anti-union initiative[1] was passed in Arizona. Cesar Chavez moved into a Phoenix barrio to begin a 24-day fast. His health was poor during the fast. He suffered from an irregular heartbeat, but he would not stop.

Chavez called for a recall of the politicians who led the fight to pass an anti-union law. His target was primarily Republican governor, Jack Williams. Chavez failed to unseat[2] the governor. But his campaign registered many new Mexican American voters. In 1974 a governor more favourable to unions was elected.

In August 1975 California got a new governor, Edmund G. Brown Jr. He was a young, pro-union politician. He put through[3] the Agricultural Labour Relations Act. The act was the first bill

---

1   initiative, *n*: 議案
2   unseat, *v*: 革除
3   put through: 使通過

of rights for farm workers ever enacted[1] in the United States. Up until this time, farm workers were not given most of the worker protections that covered people in other industries.

In a statewide election of California farm workers, the UFWOC was chosen over the Teamsters, 53 percent to 30 percent. In March 1977 the rivalry[2] between the UFWOC and the Teamsters ended. The UFWOC would represent all workers whose employers were engaged in farming.

The UFWOC under Cesar Chavez made some amazing progress by 1980. In late 1960, farm workers were lucky to be earning $2.00 an hour. By 1980, the minimum wage for farm workers was $5.00 an hour plus other benefits. By 1984, UFWOC members were earning $7.00 an hour.

---

1   enact, *v*: 通過
2   rivalry, *n*: 對抗

Cesar Chavez was still disappointed by the continued use of pesticides in the fields of California. He also disliked the living conditions for farm workers in some camps. He began another fast in July 1988. He was now sixty-one-years-old and frail.

Chavez described the fast as a way to clean his own body and soul so he could continue helping his people. He also fasted to call attention to some farm workers sickened by careless use of pesticides. Chavez pledged solidarity[1] with the weak and helpless against the proud and the powerful.

The fast was completed on August 21, after thirty-six days. Many ordinary and important people visited Chavez during the fast. When he finally ate again, Rev. Jesse Jackson, actors Danny Glover, Martin Sheen, and Edward Olmos

---

1   solidarity, *n*: 團結

joined with Congressman Peter Chacon to break bread with him. Ethel Kennedy and several of her children also came.

During this time, Cesar Chavez was alarmed about the health hazards of pesticides for farm workers. But, he also worried about how much of it was getting into the food chain*. He called it a "crisis of safety".

*Cultural Note

food chain：食物鏈，生物之間以食物營養關係，彼此聯繫起來的序列。

CHAPTER 9

Passed away 去世

As Cesar Chavez's health got worse, his daughter, Linda, became very active in the UFWOC union. She was married in 1974 to Arturo Rodriguez, who was working for the union. Over the next decades, Linda Chavez Rodriguez and her husband traveled throughout California and the nation. They were carrying out her father's cause.

In 1993 Cesar Chavez was called to Yuma, Arizona, to help UFWOC workers defend a lawsuit[1] stemming[2] from the lettuce boycott. Lettuce and vegetable grower Bruce Church, Inc. demanded the union pay large sums of money because of the money they lost during the boycott.

The lawsuit asked for millions of dollars in damages. Bruce Church, Inc. could have filed in California. But they felt they had a better chance for success filing in Arizona. The political climate was less sympathetic to unions there.

Chavez testified at the trial, looking tired and overworked. He argued that the lettuce boycott was declared legal by the California Supreme Court. After making his court appearance, Chavez drove through the neighbourhoods of Yuma where he lived as a boy. During the happy days of his early childhood, his family often drove into Yuma to go

---

1   lawsuit, *n*: 訴訟

2   stem, *v*: 起源於

to church and shop. Now, he revived old family ties and friendships.

Cesar Chavez stayed with a family in San Luis, Arizona, about twenty miles from Yuma. After his round of visiting, he returned to the concrete block home in the barrio. At 9 p.m., Chavez had dinner. He then told his hosts he was exhausted from the long questioning on the witness stand in court.

Life in the barrio was hard. The workers lived in small, crowded houses that were often shacks with no running water.
在拉美裔聚居的區域生活很艱苦，工人們需居住在偶爾暫停供水的狹窄小屋內。

So much was at stake[1]. The UFWOC union was not wealthy. An award against it for millions of dollars would be devastating[2]. Cesar Chavez was always willing to sacrifice himself for the union that he believed in so strongly.

Chavez went to bed between 10 and 10:30 p.m. that night. He was reading a book about Native Americans. The book talked about how they were trying to market the products they made on the reservations. Chavez sympathized with them. They, like the farm workers he had defended, were often stuck in poverty.

A union staff member who was also staying at the house in San Luis saw that the light in Chavez's bedroom stayed on into the night. He thought Chavez was doing what he often did, reading half the night.

---

1   at stake: 危險
2   devastating, *adj*: 極大破壞性

Although Chavez had a poor education as a child, as a man, he loved reading. The walls of his office were filled with bookshelves. He had books on philosophy, economics, labor problems, and biographies of men he admired, like Gandhi and the Kennedys.

Cesar Chavez always woke up early. He was usually out of bed by dawn to write or meditate. But, on the morning of Friday, April 23, he did not come out of the room. When union friends went to investigate, they found that Chavez had died during the night.

Chavez had never undressed, although he had taken off his shoes. He was lying on his back with an open book on Native American crafts on his chest. The book was open to the page he had apparently been reading last. He seemed to have died peacefully because any spasm[1] would have sent the book to the floor. Those who looked at Chavez said he had a contented smile on his face.

On April 29, 1993, Cesar Chavez's body arrived at the memorial park in Delano, California. That was where the funeral service was conducted. Fifty thousand people waited to pay their respects. They came from all corners of the United States, by plane, train, and car. Some of those present marched with Chavez on the road to Sacramento or in picket lines. Some had stood beside him picking walnuts, grapes, and cotton.

---

1 spasm, *n*: 抽搐

CHAPTER 10

Legacy 留下的成果

Pope John Paul II sent a statement of condolence[1] and celebration of the life of Cesar Chavez. Cardinal Roger M. Mahoney of Los Angeles called Chavez a prophet for the farm workers. Dignitaries[2] and rough-looking farm workers stood together to honor Chavez. Chavez's body lay in a simple pine coffin. The pallbearers[3] were his children, grandchildren, and people who worked with him in the fields and in the forming of the union.

---

1 condolence, *n*: 弔辭
2 dignitary, *n*: 顯要人物
3 pallbearer, *n*: 護柩者

The funeral Mass was celebrated. Then, the body of Chavez was taken to the headquarters of the UFWOC union at the field office called "Forty Acres." Chavez was buried near a bed of roses in front of his office.

Arturo Rodriguez, husband of Linda Chavez, became president of the UFWOC union. On August 8, 1994, President Bill Clinton presented Helen Chavez with the Medal of Freedom*. It was awarded after her husband's death. It is America's highest civilian honor.

Clinton praised Chavez for his nonviolent struggle to gain decent working conditions for the farm workers. Clinton described him as a "Moses figure"*. He said that Chavez had nobly and courageously led his people to a better place.

Cesar Chavez's lifestyle never changed even when he became a public figure. He never earned much money. During the entire grape strike, he and his wife and eight children lived in a rundown two bedroom, one bath, wood frame house in Delano. His enemies thought that surely the Chavez family had big bank accounts or a fine home. But this was not true.

The lawsuit from Bruce Church, Inc., which brought Chavez back to Arizona in the days before his death, was eventually thrown out[1] of court. In May 1996 Bruce Church, Inc. signed a contract with the UFWOC.

The legacy[2] of Cesar Chavez was what he had done for the Hispanic[3] and immigrant population that picked America's food. Very little was known about these people, whose hard work

---

1 throw out: 否決

2 legacy, *n*: 遺產

3 Hispanic, *adj*: 拉美裔

fed the nation. Outside of the Mexican American community, the banner with Our Lady of Guadalupe was never as well known as when it appeared in grape vineyards and lettuce fields. Chavez educated Americans about the history and traditions of Latino people. He brought home how important these hard working laborers were to America's economy.

Cesar Chavez is also important as an example of a poorly educated man with no money, who followed a bold dream and found success. He educated himself and won the hearts of millions of Americans.

On August 11, 2000, California declared March 31 as a legal holiday to celebrate the birthday and life of Cesar Chavez. Earlier, Texas had made March 31 an optional state holiday in Chavez's honor. Arizona celebrated its first official Cesar Chavez day as well in 2000.

Those who followed Chavez urged Americans to make March 31 a special kind of holiday—a "day on" instead of a "day off". They urged people to celebrate Chavez's life and work. But also, to do their part in making the world a better place like he did.

In 2003 the United States Post Office issued a stamp commemorating the strength and determination of Cesar Chavez.

美國郵政局於 2003 年發行紀念凱薩・查維斯的郵票，藉以表揚他的決心和毅力。

Exercises 練習

1. Vocabulary 詞彙

1.1 Word Ladders 字梯

按 Part 2 填入正確詞彙，改每個字 1 至 3 個字母，使它成為另一個字。請見示範。

a Catholic religious celebration — Mass
to move in front of — _____
to stop eating in protest — _____
the final one — _____

a city in California — Oxnard
not soft — _____
to do damage to something — _____
an agricultural area — farm

to get away — _____
a kind of fruit — grape
a letter on a test — _____
to be shot with a jet of liquid — _____

a restaurant server — _____
in the future — later
work — _____
the person next door — _____

1.2 Spanish in Everyday Language 日常英語的西班牙語

Part 2 出現了一些西班牙字，因為日常英語含西班牙語。先不要翻查字典，試寫下這些西班牙字的簡單定義或翻譯，看自己答對多少。

1.	chocolate	11.	chica
2.	barrio	12.	mosquito
3.	taco	13.	Colorado
4.	rancho	14.	fiesta
5.	tornado	15.	jalapeño
6.	hola	16.	bracero
7.	amigo	17.	macho
8.	patio	18.	puma
9.	burro	19.	salsa
10.	Florida	20.	tortilla

2. Understanding 理解

2.1 Acronyms 首字母縮略詞

首字母縮略詞是通過組合每個詞的首字母構成新詞，如 ASAP（As Soon As Possible）。上網或查找詞典，查出有關勞工運動和凱薩‧查維斯的縮略詞。

1. CSO _____
2. NFWA _____
3. AFL-CIO _____

4. AWOC _____

5. UFWOC _____

2.2 Everyday Acronyms 日常縮略詞

下面每個縮略詞代表甚麼？上網或查找詞典，寫出最常用的縮略詞解釋。

1. TLC _____

2. AM _____

3. TBA _____

4. PS _____

5. UFO _____

6. AKA _____

7. VIP _____

8. Your acronym:

_____

Answer Key 答案

Part 1 Mahatma Gandhi

1.1 Syllables

1. sacrifice
2. turban
3. virtuous
4. fast
5. compromise
6. convict

1.2 Label groups

1. Christians; they are all religions.
2. Manilal; they are all sons of Gandhi.
3. demonstration; they are all forms of protest.
4. Pakistan; they are all Asian countries.
5. peasants; they are all Indian castes.
6. Russia; they are all European countries involved in WWI.

2.1 Analogies 比擬

Type of analogies	Complete the analogies
1. synonyms	1. attorney : lawyer :: professor : teacher
2. descriptive	2. Gandhi : pacifist leader :: Franklin Roosevelt : president
3. whole to part	3. India : New Delhi :: U.S.A. : Washington, D.C.
4. antonym	4. war : peace :: large : small
5. item to category	5. Hinduism : religion :: Hindi : language

Part 2 Cesar Chavez

1.1 Word Ladders

Mass, pass, fast, last
Oxnard, hard, harm, farm
escape, grape, grade, sprayed
waiter, later, labour, neighbour

1.2 Spanish in Everyday Language

1. chocolate: a substance often used to make candy
2. barrio: neighbourhood
3. taco: a kind of food made with a tortilla
4. rancho: a ranch or farm
5. tornado: a wind funnel
6. hola: a greeting; hello
7. amigo: friend
8. patio: an outdoor porch
9. burro: a donkey
10. Florida: a state; meaning flowered one
11. chica: a girl
12. mosquito: a small fly
13. Colorado: a state; meaning coloured or red
14. fiesta: a party
15. jalapeño: a kind of pepper
16. bracero: legal workers from Mexico who do work that local people refuse to do; from brazo, meaning "arm" in Spanish
17. macho: male
18. puma: a large cat species
19. salsa: sauce
20. tortilla: a kind of flat bread

2.1 Acronyms

1. CSO: Community Service Organization
2. NFWA: National Farm Workers Association
3. AFL-CIO: American Federation of Labour and Congress of
   Industrial Organizations
4. AWOC: Agricultural Workers Organizing Committee
5. UFWOC: United Farm Workers Organizing Committee

2.2 Everyday Acronyms

1. TLC: Tender Loving Care
2. AM: Ante Meridien
3. TBA: To Be Announced
4. PS: Post Script
5. UFO: Unidentified Flying Object
6. AKA: Also Known As
7. VIP: Very Important Person
8. Your acronym: Example: BFF: Best Friends Forever

Proper names
專有名詞

AFL-CIO 美國勞工聯合會
及產業工會聯合會

Abdulla, Dada 阿布都拉，
達達

Afrikaners 荷裔南非人

Agricultural Labour
Relations Act
農業勞工關係法案

Agricultural Workers of
California
加州的農用工人

ambulance corps
野戰救護隊

Amritsar 阿木里查

Asiatic Law Agreement
亞裔法律協議

Bhagavad-Gita 薄伽梵歌

Birla House 柏拉屋

Black Law 黑法

Boer War 波耳戰爭

Boers 波耳人

Bombay 孟買

Braceros
墨西哥短期合同工

Brahman 婆羅門

British Empire 大英帝國

Brown, Edmond G.
布朗，埃德曼

Bruce Church, Inc
布魯士·丘奇公司

California 加州

Caste system 種姓制度

Chauri Chaura 曹里曹拉

Chavez, Ana 查維斯，安娜

Chavez, Fernando
查維斯，費南度

Chavez, Helen Fabela
查維斯，海倫·法維拉

Chavez, Juana
查維斯，胡安娜

Chavez, Librado
查維斯，利夫拉多

Chavez, Linda
查維斯，琳達

Chavez, Paul
查維斯，保羅

Chavez, Richard
查維斯，李察

Chavez, Sylvia
查維斯，塞爾維亞

Clinton, Bill
克林頓，比爾

Communist 共產主義者

Community Service
Organization (CSO)
社會服務組織

Delano, California
德拉諾市，加州

DiGiorgio Corporation
德吉奧吉奧公司

Durban, South Africa
德爾班，南非

Dyer, Gen. E. H.
戴爾將軍

Farm Security
Administration
聯邦農業安全管理局

Farm Workers Labour
Union 農場工人工會

Fresno, California
弗雷斯諾，加州

Gandhi, Devdas
甘地，達維達斯

Gandhi, Harilal
甘地，哈理拉

Gandhi, Karamchand
甘地，卡拉姆昌德

Gandhi, Kasturba
甘地，卡絲托芭

Gandhi, Laxmidas
甘地，拉斯米達斯

Gandhi, Manilal
甘地，馬尼拉

Gandhi, Putlibai
甘地，蒲立表

Gandhi, Ramdas
甘地，拉姆達斯

Glover, Danny
格洛弗，丹尼

Godse, Nathuram
高德西，南度拉姆

Government of India Act of
1919
1919 年印度政府法案

Green Boo 綠皮書

Gujarati Language
古吉拉特語

Harijans 神的子民（甘地
為賤民 Untouchable 新
取的名字）

Hartal 印度的罷工

Hitler 希特拉

Home Rule League
印度自治同盟

Huerta, Dolores
韋爾塔，多洛雷絲

Indian Franchise
印度人民選舉權法案

Indian Independence
印度獨立

Itliong, Larry
艾里昂，拉裏

Jackson, Rev. Jesse
傑克遜牧師，傑西

Jumna 贊木納河

Kennedy, Ethel
甘迺迪，埃塞爾

Kennedy, Robert
甘迺迪，羅拔

King, Coretta Scott
金，科雷塔·史葛

King, Martin Luther, Jr.
金，馬丁·路德

MacArthur, Gen. Douglas
麥克阿瑟將軍

Mahatma
印度文"大聖者"之意

Mahatma Gandhi
穆罕達默·甘地

Mahoney, Roger M.
馬洪尼，羅傑

McDonnell, Father Donald
麥克唐納，當奴神父

migrant worker 外來工

Mitchell, James
米歇爾，詹姆士

Olmos, Edward
奧爾莫斯，愛德華

Our Lady of Guadalupe
瓜達盧佩聖母

Oxnard, California
奧斯納市，加州

Phoenix 鳳凰社區

Pope John Paul II
教宗若望·保祿二世

Porbandar 柏爾本德爾

Rajkot 拉治科特

Rowlett Act 羅拉特法案

S. S. Clyde, S. S. 克萊德號

Sabarmati 沙巴馬提

Sheikh Mehtab
謝赫·麥塔布

South Africa 南非

Transvaal 特蘭斯瓦

Truth Force 真理的力量

Untouchables 賤民

Zulu 祖魯族

General Vocabulary 一般詞彙

abandon 拋棄

abolish 廢除

abusive 虐待

accordion 手風琴

add up 合計

additional 額外

ambition 抱負

ammunition 彈藥

anxious 渴望

appendicitis 盲腸炎

at stake 危險

atrocity 暴行

ballot 投票

bill 法案

blame 責備

blister 水泡

blow 打擊

bracero
墨西哥短期合同工

breach 裂痕

caste 種姓制度

ceremony 典禮

chamber pot 夜壺

charming 有魅力

chore 農莊雜務

cling to 堅持

compromise 妥協

condolence 弔辭

conquer 征服

conscience 良心

consist of 組成

content 滿足

convict 判為有罪

convince 說服

cooperate 合作

corps 隊伍

cremate 火葬

custody 監禁

customary 按慣例

cut corners 一切從簡

date 約會

datura plant 曼陀羅屬植物

day-old 隔夜

deck hand 甲板水手

deport 驅逐出境

deprive 剝奪

devastating 極大破壞性

dhoti 纏腰布

dignitary 顯要人物

discrimination 歧視

divide and conquer
分步解決

dramatic 誇張

dread 害怕

drought 乾旱時期

dues 會費

embrace a belief 信奉

enact 通過

endorse 支援

enroll 註冊

equality 平等

excommunicate 逐出

fast 絕食

fit in 適應

found 創辦

frail 體弱

garment 服裝

give birth to 誕下

grieve for 為…而悲傷

grocer 商人

hearing 聽證會

Hispanic 拉美裔

hold back 抑制

humiliate 羞辱

hymn 聖歌

indentured servants 契約僕人

independence 獨立

inferior 低等

initiative 議案新方案

insult 侮辱

intimidate 恐嚇

invade 入侵

launch 創辦發動

lawsuit 訴訟

lawsuit 訴訟

legacy 遺產

lettuce 生菜

liquor 酒

luxury 奢侈品

makeshift 臨時代用

malaria 瘧疾

margin 差數

meditate 冥想

midwife 助產士

migrant 移民

mimeograph 油印

mob 烏合之眾

morality 道德

motto 座右銘

nonviolent resistance 非暴力抵抗

null and void 無效

occasionally 偶然

occupy 佔領

ocean liner 定期遠洋客輪

on strike 罷工

pacifist 和平主義者

pallbearer 護柩者

pamphlet 小冊子

pass out 分發

paycheck 薪水

peasant 農民

penicillin 盤尼西林

persuasion 勸服

petition 請願書

pistol 任務

plead 懇求

pneumonia 肺炎

poverty-stricken 很窮

preach 講道

preacher 牧師

prevent 預防

promote 發揚

proposition 提案

pull off 靠邊

put through 使通過

pyre 火葬柴堆

rally 集會

rancher 大農場主

rebellion 反抗

recruiter 招聘人員

refugee 難民

reincarnation 轉世

resistance 反抗

rivalry 對抗敵對

rot 腐爛

rundown 破舊

sacrifice 犧牲

scavenge 在垃圾中覓食

scholar 學者

scholarship 獎學金

scripture 經文

sedition 叛亂

sentence 判刑

shock 震驚

shove 推

shrine 聖壇

sneak 偷取

sober 清醒

solidarity 團結

sorrowful 悲傷

spasm 抽搐

spin 紡織

spinning top 陀螺，美 revolving top

spiritually 精神上

spray 噴

standstill 停滯不前

stem 起源於

stern 嚴厲

stick out 凸出

stoop 屈服

strict 嚴格

struggle 奮鬥

tender 溫柔

three-storey 三層，美 three-story

throw out 否決

throw up 嘔吐

tinfoil 錫紙

tolerance 寬容

topcoat 輕便外套

tuberculosis 結核病

turban 頭巾

typhoid fever 傷寒

unseat 革除

urge 極力主張

vegetarian 素食者

victimization 犧牲

virtuous 合乎道德

vitality 活力

volunteer 志願者

walk in sb's footsteps 步某人後塵

warrior 武士

watch over 監督

widow 寡婦

windscreen 擋風玻璃，美 windshield

work out 成功

wrapper 包裝紙

Timeline of Mahatma Gandhi
穆罕達默 · 甘地年表

October 2, 1869	Gandhi was born in Porbandar, India. 甘地於印度波港出生。
1905	The "Asiatic Law Agreement" (Aka the "Black Law") was proposed, and Gandhi opposed that law and vowed a campaign of resistance called "Truth Force". 南非政府提出「亞裔法律協議」(也稱為「黑法案」)，甘地發起反抗運動「真理的力量」。
June 1914	Gandhi made an agreement with South Africa government and the Black Act was abolished. All the civil rights for Indians were returned to them. Gandhi called this a victory for his methods of peaceful resistance. 甘地與政府達成協議，廢除 "黑法案" ，印度裔居民重獲所有權利。甘地將這項勝利歸功於他的和平抗爭行動。
July 1914	Gandhi and his family returned to India. World War I broke out, Gandhi continued to oppose the war, but again he formed an ambulance corps to assist the wounded. He also asked Britain for home rule over India. He demanded an end to the untouchable class and equality for women. 甘地與家人返回印度。第一次世界大戰爆發，甘地持續反對戰爭，但同樣組織救護軍團協助傷患。他呼籲統治權回歸印度、終結賤民階級，以及婦女平權。
1920	Gandhi joined the Indian Home Rule League and became the first president. He worked tirelessly for India's independence. 甘地加入 "印度自治同盟" 成為第一任領袖，努力爭取印度獨立。

1931	Talks between Gandhi, other Indian leaders and the British fell apart. Gandhi was arrested for his political activities again. Gandhi fasted in prison and the British feared that he would die in their hands so they freed him. 甘地與其他印度領袖和英國的會談破局,甘地再次因政治行動被逮捕。甘地在獄中絕食,英國因為怕他死在英國手上而釋放他。
1939	World War II broke out, and Gandhi clung to his peaceful principles. 第二次世界大戰爆發,甘地仍舊主張不合作的和平反抗態度。
1942	Gandhi was arrested because of his theories of peaceful resistance. 英國政府因為甘地的和平反抗理論再度逮捕甘地。
May 6, 1944	Gandhi was released by the British because he suffered from malaria. It was his last prison stay. He had spent two thousand and eighty-nine days in Indian prisons and two hundred and forty-nine days in South African prisons. 甘地因罹患瘧疾而被英國政府釋放。這是甘地最後一次獄中歲月。他總共在印度監獄度過 2089 天、在南非監獄度過 249 天。
January 13, 1948	Gandhi had his final fast hoping for an end to violence. 甘地為祈求暴力終結展開最後一次絕食。
January 18, 1948	A pledge was drafted by Hindus, Muslims and others, promising tolerance for one another. Gandhi ended his fast with joy. 印度教徒、穆斯林教徒以及其他人簽下一份保證書,保證寬容對待彼此,甘地喜悦地結束絕食。
January 25, 1948	Gandhi attended a prayer meeting and was shot by Nathuram Godse. 甘地出席祈禱會時遭反對人士高德西暗殺。

March 31, 1927	Chavez was born in Yuma, Arizona. 查維斯於亞利桑那州的尤瑪市出生。
January 15, 1959	It was illegal to hire braceros if local workers were available, but the law was broken. Chavez organized a protest march of 1,500 farm workers. 雖然墨西哥短期合同工可以合法入境，聘用他們幹農活是不允許的，人們偏觸犯法律，查維斯組織了 1,500 個農工遊行抗議。
1962	Chavez had saved $1,200. With his family's support, he believed he could launch the Farm Workers Labour Union. On many grape ranches, workers had to pay for drinking water. Dangerous chemicals were frequently sprayed on the vineyards while workers were present. 查維斯積蓄了 1,200 元，得到家人支援，他相信可以組織農場工人工會。在很多兼種葡萄的大牧場，工人需要付費買水喝，即使工人在場時葡萄園會不時噴灑有害的化學藥品。
1965	The Labour Union asked people from all over California and the United States to stop buying grapes until the growers accepted the union's demands. 工會要求加州以致全美的人民罷買葡萄，直至生產商接受工會的訴求。
1967	Cesar Chavez began a fast to affirm the nonviolent nature of his struggle. 查維斯開始絕食，申明他所作努力純屬非暴力的。
July 17, 1970	Twenty-three growers were ready to negotiate. 二十三個生產商同意協商。
August 1970	Chavez was ordered to remain in jail until he agreed to end the lettuce boycott. Many famous civil rights leaders came to visit Chavez and offered their support for his cause. 查維斯被下令除非他停止抵制運送生菜，否則即須繼續關押牢房。很多著名的人權領袖都來探問查維斯，支援他堅守原則。

May 1972	Cesar Chavez suffered from an irregular heartbeat. 查維斯感不正常心跳。
July 1988	Cesar Chavez began another fast. He was now sixty-one years old and frail. 查維斯進行另一次絕食，他六十一歲，身體衰弱。
1993	Cesar Chavez was called to Yuma, Arizona, to help the Labour Union workers defend a lawsuit stemming from the lettuce boycott. The lawsuit asked for millions of dollars in damages. After making his court appearance, Chavez drove through the neighbourhood of Yuma where he lived as a boy. 查維斯被召喚到亞利桑那州的尤瑪市，幫助工會工人出庭，為禁止工人抵制生菜的行動辯護，訴訟金額達百萬元的賠償。出庭應訊後，查維斯開車經過他兒時居住尤瑪市的臨近地區。
April 23, 1993	Chavez had died peacefully during the night. 查維斯晚上平安去世。

More to Read 延伸閱讀

Arnold, David. *Gandhi*. New York: Longman, 2001.

Coolidge, Olivia. *Gandhi*. Boston: Houghton Mifflin, 1971.

Fischer, Louis. *The Life of Mahatma Gandhi*. New York: Harper and Row, 1983.

Gandhi, M.K. *Non-Violent Resistance (Satyagraha)*. Mineola, New York: Dover Publications, 2001.

Houle, Michelle, Ed. *Cesar Chavez*. San Diego: Greenhaven Press, 2003.

Matthiessen, Peter. *Sal Si Puedes*. Berkeley: University of California Press, 2000.